To: Bri~

Thanks!

Adam Baker

Maury C. Moose
and
The Forest Noel

Maury C. Moose
and
The Forest Noel

by
Adam Baker

Illustrated by Jennifer Marshall

NEW YORK

Maury C. Moose
and The Forest Noel

© 2014 Adam Baker. Illustrations, Jennifer Marshall. All rights reserved.

Published in New York, New York, by Morgan James Publishing. Morgan James and The Entrepreneurial Publisher are trademarks of Morgan James, LLC.
www.MorganJamesPublishing.com

The Morgan James Speakers Group can bring authors to your live event. For more information or to book an event visit The Morgan James Speakers Group at www.TheMorganJamesSpeakersGroup.com.

A free eBook edition is available with the purchase of this print book.

CLEARLY PRINT YOUR NAME ABOVE IN UPPER CASE

Instructions to claim your free eBook edition:
1. Download the BitLit app for Android or iOS
2. Write your name in **UPPER CASE** on the line
3. Use the BitLit app to submit a photo
4. Download your eBook to any device

ISBN 978-1-63047-054-8 paperback
ISBN 978-1-63047-055-5 eBook
ISBN 978-1-63047-076-0 hardcover

Cover Design by:
Chris Treccani
www.3dogdesign.net

Interior Design by:
Bonnie Bushman
bonnie@caboodlegraphics.com

In an effort to support local communities and raise awareness and funds, Morgan James Publishing donates a percentage of all book sales for the life of each book to Habitat for Humanity Peninsula and Greater Williamsburg

Get involved today, visit
www.MorganJamesBuilds.com

Habitat
for Humanity®
Peninsula and
Greater Williamsburg
Building Partner

Thank You!

Thank you to all of my family, friends and 89 Kickstarter backers. Without all of you, this book would not have been possible.

Introduction

Ten stops before you get to the
North Pole on the Polar Express…
You will find a magnificent forest
that's had its share of success.
It is a close knit community,
with the name of Noel…
And, boy do they have a tale to tell.
But this isn't a fantasy
with vampires or wizards…
Rather, it's an adventure with
animals like owls and lizards.
So trust me when I say that
you will remember this story…
It's about Christmas, and friendship,
and a hero named Maury.

Chapter 1

Maury C. Moose raced through the forest, dodging trees and hurtling bushes. Time was running out and if he didn't find the sleigh's missing speedometer right away, Santa would never be able to get off the ground to visit children across the world. Christmas would be ruined.

Maury could not believe that Santa's sleigh was missing the speedometer, and he was shocked to learn that he was the one animal Santa had chosen to track it down.

He was honored, but what did he know about speedometers? Didn't Santa have an army of elves that could just make a new one?

Just as Maury thought all hope was lost, he spotted the shiny speedometer floating down the river. There it was, just out of his reach in the water next to an unusual looking lily pad floating near the river bank.

But Maury's relief turned to panic as he realized that the speedometer was less than 30 feet from disappearing into the giant waterfall at the end of the river.

The speedometer would never survive if it plunged into the powerful waterfall.

With no time to waste, Maury dove into the river and lunged at the speedometer. He reached out his hoofs as far as moose-ly possible, but they came up empty.

The speedometer floated away, just out of his reach and disappeared into the waterfall.

"Noooooo!" Maury cried.

Boys and girls all across the world would not be receiving presents this year and it was all his fault. How was he going to explain this to Santa?

Suddenly, Maury was no longer in the river. His face was soaking wet but he was in his bed, and his mom was at his side.

"Is everything okay, Honey?" Carol C. Moose asked as she placed the back of her hoof against her son's antlers. "I heard you scream, so I came into your room as quickly as I could. Why are you so sweaty?"

"Mom, Christmas is ruined and it's all my fault," Maury said. "The speedometer on Santa's sleigh was missing, and he told me that I was the only one who could save Christmas. But I couldn't get to the speedometer in time, and it fell into the great waterfall. It's all my fault!"

"Oh sweetie, it was just another bad dream. Today is only December 3rd. Christmas is still three weeks away. Everything is fine, Bumpkin, let's go get you some breakfast. It's almost time for school."

Chapter 2

While Maury is asleep he can't help but stir...
For what's next, this wise moose will need
more than gold, frankincense and myrrh.

Maury was still sweating as he walked to class. This morning's dream felt so real. The forest, the trees, even splashing into the water.

Maury's imagination had always been very creative, ever since he was small.

When he was younger, dreams and a lively imagination never caused any problems. He would spend all afternoon daydreaming about becoming a movie star, the next Bullwinkle.

But in the past month, his dreams had begun to get the best of him. He had recurring nightmares about Christmas being ruined because he could not save the day.

In one dream, Prancer was sick, and Santa asked Maury to fill in, only to find out that his replacement moose couldn't move his legs.

Another time, Maury had to collect missing presents before Santa and the reindeer took off in the sleigh. The only problem was that he couldn't open his eyes wide enough to find any of the presents.

The most bizarre dream occurred when Mrs. Claus informed Maury that Jolly Old St. Nick was on a new diet and Maury had to go house to house informing all the mommies and daddies across the word that they had to bake gluten free cookies.

Would Santa really leave the fate of Christmas in the hands of an 11-year-old? Maury thought to himself as he took his seat in class. He was Rudolph's second cousin, and he did have the merriest full name in history, but saving Christmas is a lot to ask of someone who still wears hoofs-y pajamas.

"Maury?" "Maury?" "MAURY CHRIS MOOSE, can you hear me?" asked Miss L. Toad, the 5th grade teacher at Forest Noel School, interrupting Maury's thoughts on whether or not he was qualified to save Christmas.

"I'm sorry Miss Toad." said Maury. "What was the question?"

The class laughed as Miss L. Toad explained that she was taking roll.

"Do try to pay attention, Mr. Moose," said the teacher as she continued with roll call.

"Mikey Duck?"

"Present," said Maury's best friend who was also the class clown.

"Page Ant?"

"Present."

"Julie & Rob Birds?"

"Present, present."

"Justine Beaver?"

"Present."

"Simon C. Owl?"

"Present."

"Eb and Neezer Beetle?

"Yeah, we're here."

"And last, but not least, our foreign exchange student from the Holly Jolly Sea, Stock King Crab?"

"Present."

"That's eight presents and one yeah we're here. Sounds like my house on Christmas morning," joked Mikey.

Again the students laughed. "Class, before we begin today's math lesson, I have a very important announcement to make," Miss Toad said. "I regret to inform you that this year's school wide Christmas party at Jingle Bell Block has been cancelled."

What was just laughter among the students suddenly turned to shock.

"No way," blurted Mikey.

"That's impossible," said Page. "I've already picked out the dress I was going to wear."

"Please settle down class," said Miss Toad, noticing a class full of gloomy faces. "This was not my decision. I was just made aware of the cancellation this morning. If it was up to me, we would still have the party. Unfortunately, Jingle Bell Block will not be available this year."

As the kids whispered about the bad news, Maury's face went as white as the first snow of the season. He tried to pinch himself to wake up from another nightmare.

Only this time…he wasn't dreaming.

Chapter 3

The Christmas party is cancelled
and we don't know the reason…
This is going to put a damper
on Forest Noel's holiday season.

"**B**aloney! Grade A baloney. That's what this is," said Mikey as the class was dismissed. "Christmas parties and Forest Noel go together better than peanut butter and jelly beans, better than salt and peppermint, better than B-list celebrities and Dancer with the Stars."

"What could have caused the cancellation?" asked Stock.

"Maybe it's because of budget cuts," said Page.

"The rumor from the older kids is that it is a lack of Christmas spirit," added Simon.

"You are all dummies. We know the real reason that the party is being cancelled," said a voice from behind the group.

The students spun around to find Eb and Neezer Beetle smirking.

"What then?" asked Maury. "What's the real reason?"

"Our uncle is buying the land at Jingle Bell Block and turning it into a Bar Hum Bug. It is going to be a place where bugs of all shapes and sizes can go to escape the pathetic Forest Noel. The bugs are sick and tired of all the holiday cheer around here, even in the summer. Summer Christmas Camp, really? Who does that? Well, we are not going to stand for it any longer."

"No way!" shouted Justine. "The great folks of Forest Noel would never let the bugs take over Jingle Bell Block."

"Never say never," laughed Eb and Neezer as they scuttled away.

Chapter 4

Things are not good at Forest Noel…
What is now a construction site
was once the beloved Jingle Bell.

"**I** need to see this for myself," said Maury. "I can't believe the bugs would want to take over a place like Jingle Bell Block. Such a clean area doesn't seem like a good place for bugs."

To get first hand proof, the group of students walked to Jingle Bell Block. As the kids climbed over Wreath Mountain and looked down on the Block, they couldn't believe their eyes.

"That's JB Block?" asked Page.

"We must have gone the wrong way," said Justine. "I don't remember there being trash everywhere."

"This place is a dump. A grade-A dump," said Mikey. "I've swam in sewers that are cleaner than this place."

"For someone who gets straight C's, you sure seem to know a lot about things being grade-A," joked Simon.

"When did this happen?" asked Maury. "My family has been coming here since before I grew antlers and I've never seen it this bad. I guess we haven't been here since the new 'Deck The Mall' was built across town, but not in my wildest dreams did I think it could get this bad around here."

As the group discussed how this could have happened, Maury thought back to all the years he visited JB Block. The giant Christmas tree in the middle of the block, when fully decorated, lit up the town like a city of fireflies. Now the tree looked like an abandoned building in the center of a dump.

"What is G.R. Inchworm Construction?" said Julia, pointing to an ugly green sign posted into the ground that read "FUTURE SITE OF BAR HUM BUG" in big letters.

"That must be Eb and Neezer's uncle's company," answered Rob. I bet he's the one who is trying to take over this land so he can build that bug bar. According to the sign the land will be his in 12 days."

"Maybe we can talk to him and ask if he will take his construction project to another town," said Page. "We just need to explain to him how much JB Block means to everyone."

"Yeah right," said Mikey. "If he is anything like Eb & Neezer then I'm sure he is a real joy to talk to. There is only one of us who could possibly convince him to leave the Block alone. For this job we are going to have to throw a Hail Maury!"

With that, all eyes slowly turned to the largest one in the group.

Chapter 5

It appears that Jingle Bell Block
will be replaced by a bar...
In this time of trouble the desperate group
looks up to its North Star.

Maury couldn't help but feel the heat of 14 eyes firmly focused on his six foot frame.

"What is everybody looking at?" Maury playfully asked. Do I have a booger in my nose or something?"

"Yes, but that is not why we are looking at you this time," replied Mikey. "Unless you plan to use those boogers to scare G.R. Inchworm away from Jingle Bell Block."

"Come on guys," Maury said as he wiped his nose. "I am not the Moose for the job. Why me? What do I have that you don't?"

"Boog---"

"Enough with the boogers," Justine interrupted Mikey. "Beside the size, the brains and the merriest full name ever, I guess you have nothing on us. Seriously, Maury, you are the only one of us who stands a chance to convince G.R. Inchworm to leave."

"Just tell him about the upcoming Christmas party and how it is an annual school tradition. Explain that Christmas will be ruined if he builds his bar."

"Let him know about the memories JB Block has made for all of us," added Page. "Like the time our 1st grade class took a field trip to the block to go ice skating and the rink didn't have skates small enough for me. So you let me sit on your antlers as we raced around the rink, chasing after Mikey. After he hears about how much this place means to us, he will surely move his bar somewhere else."

"Yeah, and if that touching story doesn't work, you can just squish him with your giant feet," said Mikey.

"Fine, I will go talk to G.R.," said Maury. "But I'm going to need back up."

Chapter 6

Our hero, the moose,
is off to talk to the worm…
A task so daunting, it would make
even Rudolph squirm.

Maury's knees were shaking so much he could hardly walk in a straight line as he and Mikey approached G.R. Inchworm Construction headquarters.

The place reeked of rotten eggs and had a look that not even three blind mice could love. And that was just from the outside.

Maury and Mikey plugged their noses as they entered.

"What do you two want?" snapped a roach at the receptions desk.

"W-W-We'd like to see Mr. Inchworm," stuttered Maury.

"Ha! No chance," said the female receptionist as she turned back to the New York Slimes newspaper she was reading. "Mr. I. doesn't want to be bothered."

"Can't we just see him for a few seconds?" pleaded Maury. "We will not take long."

"No way. The great G.R. Inchworm has much better things to do than meet with you two lousy kids."

Maury turned to leave when Mikey shouted, "Well these two lousy kids have a stink bomb, and if we don't get to see Mr. I. immediately we will be forced to shoot…uh, I mean detonate this smelly thing."

The receptionist put down the newspaper. "Oh yeah? Where's the stink bomb?"

"Let's just say, if I lift up my right wing, this whole place will smell worse than Maury's feet after basketball practice."

"What are you doing?" Maury whispered to Mikey.

"Just go with it."

"Oh, uh, yeah, you don't want that. My feet can get very stinky. Just ask my mom. She hates doing my laundry after basketball practice." said Maury.

At this point, the roach behind the front desk was already reading the newspaper again and clearly did not want to be bothered, stink bomb or no stink bomb. "Honey, you are in the wrong place if you think a stink bomb is going to scare anyone. But I'm tired of dealing with you, so I am going to let you see Mr. Inchworm. It's the third door on the left. We will see who drops the bomb."

Mr. Inchworm was on the phone as Maury and Mikey entered the gigantic, moldy office.

"I've sleepwalked into better deals than this. I don't care what the Ogre Swamp costs. JUST BUY IT!" yelled G.R Inchworm as he slammed down the phone, knocking over the larva lamp on his desk. "Who let you back here?"

"Your lovely receptionist," answered Mikey.

"What do you want?" asked an irritated G.R.

"Go for it, Maury," said Mikey, quickly backing away and hiding behind his much larger pal.

"M-Mr. Inchworm, sir. W-W-We came here to talk to you about your construction project at Jingle Bell Block," said Maury. "We wanted to see if you would move it to a different location."

"HAHAHAHA," laughed G.R. "This has to be a joke. Am I on an episode of Skunk'd? Where are the hidden cameras?"

"No joke, sir," said Maury, his heart racing. "We just thought you'd like to know how much the Block means to Forest Noel. Our school holds the annual Christmas party there, and animals throughout the forest do not want to see the land changed."

"Listen here, son, if you think I am just going to walk away from a goldmine just so you and your friends can have your silly little Christmas party, then you aren't the brightest bulb on the Christmas tree," G.R. barked.

"In 12 days the land will be mine and you can kiss your beloved Jingle Bell Block goodbye. And after I own the block, I'm coming after the rest of your Forest Noel, or as I like to call it, NO WELL. Now why don't you and your feathered friend get out of my office IMMEDIATELY!"

Chapter 7

Maury and Mikey's plan had failed...
If they don't come up with something fast,
their Polar Express will be derailed.

Maury and Mikey's walk from G.R. Construction back to the group felt as cold and as long as a winter snowstorm. Maury kept replaying G.R.'s cynical laugh over and over again in his head.

This feels just like a bad dream, if not worse, Maury thought to himself as they approached their classmates.

"How did it go?" asked Julia

"Yes, what did he say?" asked Rob. "Did he agree to let us keep the land?"

"Let's just say, we bombed," said Mikey.

"Maury, you look like you just ate something sour," said Simon. "Is everything okay?"

"I'm really, really sorry guys, but I let you down," Maury said. "G.R. isn't going to leave. In fact, he said he plans to take over the rest of Forest Noel after he is finished with JB Block. I just couldn't change his mind...I failed."

"No, you didn't fail. You didn't let us down," said Justine.

"Yeah, Maury, I'm sure you did better than any of the rest of us could have done," said Page.

"I still say you should have just squished him," joked Mikey.

"What do we do now?" asked Simon.

The group stood silent as no one knew the answer to Simon's question. Then Maury spoke first.

"G.R. said in 12 days the land will be his and JB Block as we know it will be destroyed. Unless anyone knows how to stop a rich and powerful worm, I am not sure what we can do."

"Does anyone have a giant can of Bug-Be-Gone?" asked Mikey.

"Come on Mikey, that isn't funny," said Page. "Our forest is at risk, and I don't think this is a time for jokes."

"How do you stop an evil inchworm and his army of bugs?" asked Justine.

"I don't think he can be stopped," Maury said, dejected as he walked away from the group, alone.

Chapter 8

All seems to be lost and it appears
that G.R. Inchworm has won...
The group breaks apart, with seemingly
nothing left to be done.

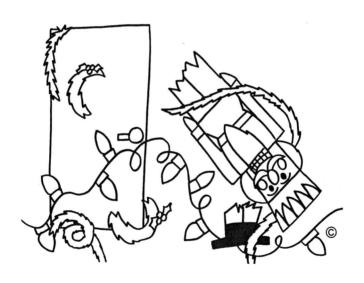

Maury walked home in a haze. He couldn't stop thinking about Christmas, G.R. Inchworm and how he let his friends down. Mentally and physically exhausted, he went straight into his room and flopped down on his bed, hoping to forget the previous few hours.

Closing his eyes, Maury tried to ignore the shining colorful lights and dozens of festive decorations dangling throughout his room. But he couldn't put them out of his mind. Looking at them brought him back to this afternoon when he was embarrassed in front of his friends.

Not feeling the Christmas spirit, Maury popped out of his bed and pulled the Christmas lights off of his walls. He tore down the tinsel that was hung around his doorway. He busted the wreath hanging on his closet door and snapped the nutcracker next to his bed.

Maury knew what he was doing was wrong, but G.R Inchworm was ruining Christmas and he no longer wanted to have all the ornaments in his room.

As he moved toward the miniature Christmas tree in the corner of his room, there was a knock at the door.

"Go away, mom," Maury yelled toward the door. "I want to be left alone right now."

"Supper is ready, Bumpkin," replied a young voice behind the door. "And I've made your favorite…fried worm."

Confused, Maury opened the door to find Mikey.

"Looks like someone has redecorated," said Mikey. "Going for the post-tornado look?"

"What do you want Mikey? I'm not in the mood for jokes."

"Sorry dude, just trying to lighten the mood," said Mikey as he picked up the broken nutcracker. "Looks like this guy has seen better days."

"I know how he feels," said Maury.

"Do you remember when we were six, and we were going to our first Summer Christmas Camp?" asked Mikey.

"Yes, but I don't see what that has to do with my broken nutcracker."

"I was so scared about being away from my family for two weeks that I did everything thing I could think of to get out of camp," continued Mikey. "I pretended to have bird flu, swine flu, any type of flu I could think of just so they would send me home early. But they just wouldn't let me leave. Then you showed me that camp was so much fun and that I would be back with my family before I knew it. You told me not to be afraid and look at the fun we would have instead of what I was missing at home. You showed me how to turn what I thought was a bad situation into the best two weeks of my life."

"What's your point?" asked Maury. "Are you saying I should use the knots we learned back at camp and tie G.R. Inchworm into a bow tie?"

"That wasn't what I was going for, but that is actually not a bad idea. Let's try a different example...Remember when we were in kindergarten and Eb and Neezer used to pick on me every day? They called me the "ugly duckling's even uglier little brother." Well, you stood up to them for me. I was too scared to do anything, but you were brave and told them to leave me alone or else you would blacken their already black eyes. When I asked you why you did that, do you remember what you said?"

"No."

"You said, 'that's what friends do. They stand up for one another, especially when times are tough.' Well now it is my time to return the favor. We only have 12 days left before our town is taken over by a bunch of rotten bugs. Times are as tough as I can ever remember, but I will not let us give up now. I know we can save JB Block, but I'm going to need your help. Are you in?"

"Fine, I am in."

"That was not very convincing. Say it like you mean it. Or would you rather live in a forest ruled by bugs??"

"I'm in, or else my name isn't Maury Chris Moose!"

"Great, now let's go practice those bow tie knots."

"I've got a better idea," said Maury. "Round up the gang and let's meet at the school. Your story of summer camp reminded me of how we can get some answers on how to stop G.R."

Chapter 9

New courage builds in Maury
as he forms a plan of attack...
All thanks to Mikey, a great friend,
even if he is a quack.

Night was just beginning to fall as the group of students met outside of Forest Noel School. Nervous tension mixed with a sense of building excitement as they waited to hear Maury's plan.

"Maury, what do you have in mind?" Simon asked. "All Mikey said to do was to meet here and something about a bow tie knot."

"When we all were in summer camp, do you remember how the counselors would tell campfire stories about the magical lily pad?" asked Maury.

"The one that could answer any question?" said Page.

"Exactly," said Maury. "They talked about the legend of the magical lily pad that knew the answer to any question. Well, now we are questioning how to deal with an evil inchworm. All we need to do is find that lily pad and it will tell us how we can stop G.R."

"That's great, Maury, but we don't even know if that thing is real," said Justine. And, even if it is, we have no idea how to find it."

"That is true, but I had a dream the other night where I dove into the Yuletide River, and, just before I hit the water, I spotted a strange looking lily pad tucked up against the river bank. I didn't think about it then, but it looked so much like what the campers would describe that it has to be the magical one."

"I guess it's worth a try," said Mikey. "I could use a swim."

"Great! Follow me."

The group felt a new purpose as they followed their leader to the river.

Maury remembered the exact route he took in his dream when he was looking for Santa's missing speedometer. Finally, the vividness of his dreams was paying off.

Following Maury's lead, the group raced along the river to the north side of the forest. Zigging and zagging through the evergreen trees, Maury did not stop until he came upon a large apple tree on the edge of the river. He cautiously approached the river bank, unsure of what exactly he was going to find.

"In my dream the pad was just past this giant apple tree," said Maury, leading the group toward the tree that was covered in juicy red apples, which was an extremely rare sight in December.

"Is that it?" yelled Page, pointing to something floating in the water.

"You mean that glassy metallic floating thingy?" said Mikey.

"Yes, that's it," said Maury. "That is what I saw in my dream."

As Maury got close to the water he realized that the magic lily pad was just far enough away in the water that he couldn't reach.

"Mikey, this job was made just for you," he said, looking at his webbed footed friend.

"CAAANNNONN BAAALLLLL!" Mikey yelled as he splashed into the water.

"Be careful," said Simon. "You don't know what to expect with that thing."

"Careful is my middle name," said Mikey, who was already climbing onto the six foot long pad. "How do you get this thing to work? What did your dream say about that, Maury?"

"I didn't try to use it in my dream. I woke up before I realized it was magic."

"Maybe it needs a good jolt!" said Mikey, jumping into the air and landing near the edge of the pad.

As soon as he landed, the pad lit up like a Christmas tree, causing the group to cover their eyes.

"I guess that worked," Mikey said. "Now what?"

"Ask it a question," said Maury.

"Are you a magical lily pad?" asked Mikey

Just as Mikey got the words out of his mouth, the pad made two quick beeping noises.

"Yes, I am magic, but it is pronounced Lil-Eye-Pad," said the floating device in a robotic female voice. "My name is Sure-y."

The pad then beeped twice again and was silent.

"Hi Sure-y. I'm Mikey. Sorry I was jumping around on your face."

"Sure-y, my name is Maury. We have come here to seek your help," Maury yelled from the river bank.

Two more quick beeps and Sure-y said, "How may I assist you, Maury?"

"We need to know how to get G.R. Inchworm to leave Jingle Bell Block," said Maury.

Another two beeps and the pad spoke, "I have three different routes to get to G.R. Inchworm Construction from Jingle Bell Block."

"Directions, why would we come to a magic floating pad for directions?" said Mikey. "I think this thing is broken."

"Quiet Mikey," said Maury. "I remember the counselors saying that the magic pad was a little tricky and you had to ask direct questions. Try a more specific question, Mikey."

"How do we save Christmas?" Mikey asked Sure-y.

Beep beep, "I'm showing 3,000 results for how to save Christmas," answered Sure-y.

"Great, this should be easy then," said Mikey. "What is the first of the 3,000?"

Beep beep, "To save Christmas you must use three ghosts to cause the villain to have a change of heart," said Sure-y. "The ingredients call for one ghost from the past, one ghost from the present and one from the future."

"Seriously?" said Mikey. "That's crazy. Even if we did find three ghosts, there is no way something like that would ever work. We are trying to save Christmas, not Halloween."

"Ask it how to get rid of an inchworm," said Maury.

"Sure-y, let's pretend that we don't have three ghosts. How do we get rid of an inchworm?" Mikey asked.

After two more beeps, Sure-y spoke again. "Inchworms and other bugs do not like the following: clean areas, fresh trees, and nice odors."

"That information would be great if we were writing a bug report," Mikey said sarcastically. "But how does that help us when we only have 12 days until Christmas is ruined?"

Beep beep, "12 days of Christmas," spoke Sure-y. "12 drummers drumming, 11 pipers piping, ten lords-a-leaping, nine ladies dancing, eight maids-a-milking, seven swans-a-swimming, six geese-a-laying, five gold rings, four colly birds, three French hens, two turtle doves, and a partridge in a pear tree."

"We already know that song, Sure-y," said Mikey.

"Wait just a second!" shouted Maury. "Worms hate clean areas…drummers drumming. Sure-y, you are a genius!"

"How the heck did you come to that conclusion?" asked a puzzled Mikey as he jumped off the Lil-Eye-Pad and swam back to meet the gang.

Chapter 10

The group looks at their leader
like he has a screw loose…
But fear not, dear reader, you
can count on Maury C. Moose.

"**Y**eah, what are you talking about, Maury?" asked Stock.

"Sure-y said that inchworms don't like things that are clean," said Maury. That's why G.R. wants to take over JB Block. It has become a dump. We didn't take care of it and now it is the perfect place for bugs. But I bet if we clean it up and make it smell nice and fresh again, with new trees, the bugs will not want to visit a bar there."

"What about drummers drumming?" asked Justine. "Sure-y didn't say anything about worms hating Christmas songs."

"Not drummers drumming or pipers piping," said Maury. "In our case it will be plumbers plumbing and wipers wiping."

"What about lords-a-leaping?" asked Mikey. "What's your rhyme for that one, Dr. Smoose?"

"I don't know…forest-a-keeping? I don't have one for all 12," replied Maury.

"Darn, I was really looking forward to what you could come up with for ladies dancing," laughed Mikey.

"Seriously guys," said Maury. We have 12 days to clean up JB Block and get rid of the bugs. I won't be able to do it without your help."

"I'm in," said Justine Beaver. "I come from a long line of plumbers."

The rest of the group followed with their support. "You guys are the best," Maury said. "Operation Jingle Bell Rock starts tomorrow after school."

Chapter 11

A plan has been formed and
G.R. doesn't know what's coming...
Thanks to the magic of Sure-y
and 12 drummers drumming.

Maury couldn't focus on a thing Miss L. Toad taught in school the next day. Class was a blur as the gang couldn't wait to clean up JB Block. When the final bell rang, the group gathered near the playground.

"I think the first step is to scout out JB Block and see what G.R. has planned," said Maury. "Once we figure out exactly what we are up against we will have a better idea of what needs to be done."

The group agreed and made their way to Jingle Bell Block. But they weren't the only ones.

An old yule log provided a perfect hiding place as Maury, Mikey, Justine, Simon, Page, Stock, Julia and Rob sat less than 100 feet from the G.R. Inchworm Construction sign. Despite the fact that G.R. did not yet own the land, he had guard bugs protecting his soon to be property.

"Looks like a total of eight guards," Simon said. "He must be serious about this land and his Bar Hum Bug. And no wonder, this place is a dump. Just look at how comfortable the guards seem here."

"Creating a dam on the river bank and getting rid of all this water should be our first step," said Justine. "That should solve the irrigation problem and make it easier to clean up the trash."

"Great idea, Justine," said Maury. "Once the water is gone we will need to pick up all the dead branches and clear out the garbage so we have room to plant new trees. Simon, Julia, Rob, do you think you can handle that?"

"No problem," answered the three birds.

"Finally, once the ground is cleared, Page, Mikey and I can plant new trees," said Maury. "You still have those magic beans, don't you Mikey?"

"Of course I do. I always knew the golden goose side of my family would come in handy," answered Mikey as he thought about how his distant relatives whose adventures with a guy named Jack and his giant beanstalk were going to come in handy.

"That's perfect," said Maury. Let's come back at 11 o'clock tonight when the guards have gone home and no one is around."

As the group turned to leave they were stopped by the one, two punch of doom and gloom.

"What do you think you guys are doing?" asked Eb.

"Yeah," added Neezer. "Why are you snooping around here?"

"We were just leaving," said Maury.

"You better leave," said Neezer. "And we don't want to see you here anymore."

"That's good," said Mikey. "We don't really want to see you anymore either."

As the Moose and his pals left, Eb turned to his brother and said, "They were up to something. We better go tell Uncle G.R. about this."

Chapter 12

As the group forms the plan,
Eb and Neezer happen to see...
When these beetles come together and get a little
help from their friends, they just won't let it be.

"**H**i, Auntie," Ed and Neezer said as they entered the G.R. Inchworm Construction headquarters.

"Hey, boys, what's up?" said the roach at the reception desk, as she put down her Pus Weekly magazine.

"We came to see Uncle G.R.," said Eb. "We have to tell him something about a moose from school."

"Would that be the same mangy moose and duck that came by here a few days ago?"

"That's them," said Neezer. "And they are up to something. So we came to warn Uncle G.R."

"Go right ahead."

The boys made their way back to their uncle's office, first stopping to check out the pictures on the hallway wall of their uncle with famous celebrities. The boys were in awe as they passed by a picture of G.R. on stage with Justin Timber Snake. Another picture showed off G.R shooting hoops with Kobe Bry Ant. The last picture was from a meeting G.R. had with Mark Zuker Bug.

"Uncle G.R., Uncle G.R., we have something very important to tell you," they shouted as they burst into the room.

G.R. was on the phone and put a finger to his mouth to quiet the boys down. "Face Bug is going to be a worldwide phenomenon, and if you try to get in my way I will crush you!" he said as he hung up the phone.

"What is it boys? I'm very busy."

"We came to warn you that Maury Chris Moose and his friends are going to try and stop you from taking over Jingle Bell Block," said Eb.

"His name is Maury Chris Moose? No wonder he is crazy about Christmas."

"Just crazy if you ask me," said Neezer. "We couldn't get their exact plan, but we overheard them say something about drummers drumming and pipers piping tonight. We think they are planning to sing you Christmas carols or something."

"Maybe they think their horrible voices will scare you away," said Eb.

"Whatever they have planned, they won't get away with it," said G.R. "If that no good moose thinks he can stop me, then he has another thing coming. Thanks for the warning boys. Now get out of my office! I've got some work to do. Before I deal with that Moose I've got to foreclose on that widow's farm on the other side of town."

Chapter 13

Looks like G.R. Inchworm has
something up his sleeve…
It's going to take a group effort
to get this Scrooge to leave.

A s Maury's mother tucked him into bed, he glanced at his Sponge Bob Square Ants wall clock. 9:45 p.m. Just enough time.

"Good night, Sweetie," said his mother as she kissed him on the forehead. "Don't let the bed bugs bite."

Bed bugs, Maury thought to himself. More like bad bugs.

Maury laid his head on his pillow as his mom turned out the light and closed the door.

Maury waited silently in the darkness for the sound of his mother's hoofsteps to disappear out of the hallway and into the living room. He knew that when she left his room she would go out to the couch and join his father to watch their favorite TV show, Two and a Half Moose.

Once the hallway was still, Maury clicked on the small flash light he was hiding under his Milwaukee Bucks sheets. The flashlight provided enough light for him to put his fake Maury in place, just in case his mom or dad decided to check on him when he was gone.

Tiptoeing out of bed, Maury made his way to the closet. He sifted through Christmas sweaters his grandparents had sent him but he never wore, until he found exactly what he was looking for.

While he took the tattered red coat with built in padding and matching suspenders, he thought back to all the use this suit had gotten through the years. Whether it was a Halloween costume or the outfit he wore when he starred in the school's Christmas play, his Santa costume had definitely been worth the money he spent on it three years ago. Now it was on its last leg and a bit too small for him, but tonight's use would be its most important ever.

Maury silently walked back to his bed and lifted up the covers. He slid the Santa costume under the sheets and fluffed up the padding to form what looked like a sleeping moose.

Looking good, he thought to himself. But not quite ready.

He turned to his dresser, reaching beyond his school spirit award and his Christmas card collection, all the way to the back where he grabbed the most crucial part of the night's disguise.

Holding up the flashlight, he looked at the hat with moose antlers he had won at the Rocky and Bullwinkle theme park.

Maury placed the antler-hat on his pillow and pulled up the sheets just enough to cover the brim of the hat.

As he took a step back to admire his handiwork, Maury smiled. He normally would not sneak out of his room, but desperate times called for desperate mooses.

If his mom or dad peeked into his room, they would see what looked like a sound asleep moose tucked snugly in bed. The first step of the plan was finished, but the hard part was yet to begin. Maury quietly climbed out his window, off to meet his friends at JB Block.

Chapter 14

The room is dark and a fake Moose
is asleep in the bed...
No rest for Maury, as he chose
to save Christmas instead.

A cold wind blew through the tall trees as the group met just outside of Jingle Bell Block. A full moon lit up the forest but also gave a spooky feeling to this silent night.

As the group made their way to the edge of JB Block they saw something that made their feet, and almost their hearts, stop.

"Is that what I think it is?" Simon asked.

"I'm afraid so," answered Maury. "Looks like G.R. Inchworm is guarding his land. But why tonight? It's almost like he knew we were coming."

"I bet his scumbag nephews spied on us and tattled," said Mikey.

"How are we going to clean up the forest now?" Julia asked.

"Yeah Maury, G.R. will surely hear us," added Rob.

"I'm afraid it gets worse," said Stock, who was staring at the sleeping worm. "Look at the for sale sign. The "12 days" before G.R. takes control of the land has been crossed out and replaced with two days. We might be too late."

Maury could see the devastated look on his friends' faces. He knew that he had to say something, but he didn't know what. "Don't worry guys. We will think of something. Let's scrap the plan for tonight and meet after school to come up with a new plan."

The next day, class was the last thing on Maury's mind. He had to come up with a way to stop G.R. from sleeping in JB Block. He just had to. He racked his brain all day long but could not come up with any good ideas. Maybe someone else in the group will come up with something when we meet after school, he thought.

However, the meeting at the playground did not start very promising.

"No one has any ideas on how we can get rid of G.R. for a night?" Maury asked the group.

"I still thi---"

"Besides stepping on him, Mikey," Maury interrupted before his sarcastic friend could finish his joke.

"What if we made soothing noises?" said Julia and Rob. "Our mom did that for us when we couldn't fall asleep when we were little."

"Good suggestion, guys," said Maury. "But unfortunately I don't think that worms find chirping bird noises as soothing as baby birds do."

"We should go back to Sure-y and see if she has anymore answers," suggested Stock.

"No way!" said Mikey. "That floating pad makes me want to wear my grandmother's Christmas earmuffs and plug my ears."

"What did you just say?" asked Maury.

"That Sure-y makes my ears hurt," said Mikey.

"No, the part about covering your ears with earmuffs. That's it!" exclaimed Maury.

"What's it?" asked a confused Mikey.

"We don't have to remove G.R. from JB Block tonight, we just have to remove his hearing, so we can go about our plan without him waking up."

"Good idea, pal, but I don't think my grandmother will let us use her Christmas earmuffs," said Mikey. She guards those things like a prized possession."

"Not earmuffs, headphones," said Maury. "I know a doctor who makes noise cancelling headphones out of vegetables."

Vegetables? The group thought to themselves. How do you make headphones out of vegetables?

But they didn't have time for Maury to explain. He took off running, and everyone quickly followed.

After a half a mile, Maury finally stopped running just outside of an oversized doghouse. The group entered through the front door that had a sign hanging above it that read, "Dr. Dreidel's Headphones."

"Maury, it is great to see your face. It's been so long since I've seen you in this place," said a large black dog behind the counter.

"Doc, it's great to see you too," said Maury. "I'm sorry, but we are short on time. I need to see your best headphones."

The doctor grabbed a pair off the top shelf and said, "Of course, my dear friend, if the best is what you seek, look no further than the Beets special edition that cancels all sound. It eliminates more noise than if you put your head underground."

"Perfect," said Maury as he grabbed the headphones and read the package. Beets headphones, light as a feather, rated #1 vegetable headphone in the world.

"Thanks, Doc." Maury said after paying for the headphones and leading the group out of the doghouse.

"All we have to do is slip these headphones on G.R. tonight and then we will be able to clean up JB Block just like we had planned."

"Are you sure he won't be able to hear us?" asked Page.

"It's our only hope," answered Maury. "We have to try this tonight or JB Block will be gone forever."

Chapter 15

'Twas the night of the cleaning
but no one was loose...
All stomachs were stirring,
even the gut of our moose.

"**S**weet dreams," said Carol C. Moose as she tucked in her son and closed his bedroom door.

When it came to saving Christmas, Maury hadn't had good luck with dreams. He prayed that tonight would be different, but a part of him just wanted to stay in bed.

But he knew he couldn't. The gang was counting on him. Heck, the whole forest was counting on him. He had to try. Even if he failed, he was not going down without putting up a fight.

Despite the watermelon sized butterflies in his stomach, Maury pulled himself out of bed and began to put together his fake sleeping moose.

After a few minutes, Maury once again admired his handiwork. It sure looked like a snoozing moose was in his bed, but something about the rest of his room was not right.

He hadn't cleaned up since his "redecorating" the other day, and since there was a chance this would be his last Christmas, he needed to make sure his room was filled with holiday cheer.

He grabbed the Christmas lights off of the floor and pulled the tinsel out of the trash. As quietly as a mouse, he hung the colorful lights back on the ceiling and placed the twinkling tinsel around the door.

Last, but not least, he took a glue stick and repaired the destroyed nutcracker and wreath. As he placed the repaired nutcracker back on his nightstand, he got a whiff of his wreath's cinnamon aroma. This might just come in handy tonight, Maury thought as he placed the wreath securely around his antler, grabbed his knapsack and climbed out of his window.

Chapter 16

Maury's room is repaired
and filled with holiday spirit…
To save Christmas, he will have to work
quietly so the evil bug doesn't hear it.

Unlike the previous night, the moon was only half full. This made the forest even spookier, and it also made things harder to see.

The darkness might give us an advantage, Maury thought to himself as he met the rest of the group.

Once again, G.R. was sleeping in the middle of JB Block. Only this time, they were ready.

Maury pulled Dr. Dreidel's Beets out of his knapsack and turned to Simon.

"Simon, you are used to being out at this time of night. That makes you our X-factor. Think you can get these around G.R.'s ears without him waking up?"

"It would be my pleasure," Simon said not wasting any time to grab the veggie headphones.

As Simon soared into the night sky, the group held their breath. This was only step one, but if the bug woke up from this, their plan would be foiled before it even began.

Simon landed in an old tree less than twenty feet from where G.R. slept. Taking one last look at G.R., the owl crept off of the tree branch and slowly began his descent, using his powerful wings to hover silently in the air.

He slowly floated down and down until he was just a foot from the sleeping worm. Simon gripped the headphones with his beak, squinting to line up the beets directly above G.R.'s head. He then took one final breath and released the headphones.

Time stood still as the beets softly fell over the ears of G.R.

Simon pumped his wings in celebration as step one was complete. When he returned to the group, the kids exchanged high fives.

"That was amazing," said Stock.

"Yeah, I really didn't think you could do it," Mikey joked. "I was already hiding because I thought G.R. would hear you."

Now that the sleeping worm could not hear a thing, it was time for Operation Jingle Bell Rock.

"Just remember our version of the 12 Days of Christmas," said Maury. "Justine, you and Stock will be in charge of the plumbing. "Julia, Rob and Simon will do the sweeping. Page and Mikey, you come with me. We will take care of the pair of trees, minus the partridge."

And just like that, the group was off in every direction.

Stock and Justine scampered to the middle of the block where water had overflowed from the river and created a swamp. Stock used his powerful claws to quickly dig trenches in the ground to create a drainage system. The drainage lines began at the middle of the block where the most water had built up, and extended directly to the river.

As Stock and Justine pushed the water back to the river, Julia, Rob and Simon flew around, collecting the broken branches and piles of trash that littered the forest. They loaded them up in their beaks and flew them to the bank of the river. Justine used the branches and sticks to create a wall on the river bank to stop the water from overflowing.

Once the water stopped flooding into the block, Justine joined Stock and the two of them continued to dig trenches to help get rid of the excess water and dry out the land.

While all this was going on, Maury, Mikey and Page marked off areas to plant the new evergreen trees. Thanks to the help of the magic beans, the trees would be full size by morning. But the seeds had to be planted far enough away from one another so they wouldn't grow into each other and be uprooted.

Maury used his hoofs to mark off 12 holes, each 25 feet away from one another. He then gave the beans to Page who tunneled deep into the ground to deposit the magic. Mikey took water from Stock and Justine's drainage system and carried it in his bill so he could pour it on top of each of the holes. Once Page was out of the holes, Maury covered them up with dirt and patted down the ground.

Just like that, trees were already growing and the forest was beginning to look new again. But there was still a smell that would embarrass a skunk.

Maury was just about to pull an air freshener out of his knapsack when a noise came from the direction of G.R.

Fear rippled through Maury's body as G.R. stood up.

"Stay still," Maury whispered to the group. "It may be dark enough that he won't see us."

Maury's eyes stayed focused on the inchworm as he walked over to one of the sprouting new trees. Something was different. Instead of G.R.'s confident, even cocky walk, he was instead slowly walking upright, like a mummy.

G.R. stopped at the budding tree and said, "Hello, Mr. Tree. Would you like to come to my bar?"

"What do we do?" asked Page.

"Keep still," said Maury, his heart still pounding with fear. "I think he is sleepwalking. Hopefully it won't be long before he lies back down."

"Not much of a talker, Mr. Tree?" said the sleepwalking worm to the now bigger tree. "I don't feel like talking much either. You seem soft, mind if I lay down here?"

And just like that, G.R. was out again, asleep next to the tree.

"Okay, I think he is down," said Maury. "Did everyone bring their air fresheners?"

The group all nodded.

"We brought cinnamon eggnog scent," said Julia and Rob.

"I brought peppermint," said Simon.

"I have candy cane," said Page.

"Gingerbread cookie scent for us," said Stock and Justine.

"I brought a scent of something my mom always makes for me when I am sick," said Maury. "NativiTea. What about you Mikey?"

"New car smell!"

"New car smell, really?" asked Maury.

"Oh yeah," Mikey said. "Have you ever seen a worm drive a new car?"

"I guess you have a point," said Maury. "Now let's hang these scents everywhere we can. Once we cover up this rotten egg odor we can get out of here."

At that, the gang scattered and when they got back together, the block smelled drastically different. The new trees smelled like a new car that was filled with a tea, cinnamon, peppermint, candy cane, and gingerbread cookie aroma.

"One last thing," Maury said to the group as they began to leave. He took the wreath off of his antlers and hung it around the for sale sign.

"Perfect."

Chapter 17

The work is done and JB Block
looks like a whole new place...
When he wakes up, we can't wait
to see the look on G.R.'s face.

G.R. woke up dazed and confused, as was the case every time he sleepwalked. Only this time he was even more puzzled. He had gone to sleep at the run down Jingle Bell Block, home of his future bar. However, he had awoken in a foreign place filled with fresh trees.

How far did I sleepwalk, he thought to himself as he tried to shake the cobwebs out of his head. I must have gone up hill because my ears are plugged, and I can't hear a thing.

Where am I? This is nothing like JB Block. I am glad I am not buying this place. Bugs would never come here.

Wiping the sleep from his eyes, G.R. noticed something familiar. His jaw dropped to the floor when he saw a cocoon tent between two giant evergreen trees. The tent looked exactly like the one he had brought to Jingle Bell Block the night before.

Was it possible that he sleepwalked and brought his tent with him? Possible, but not likely. He probably would have tripped and woken up if he tried to carry a tent while sleepwalking.

Was it possible that he was still in JB Block?

There's no way. This looked nothing like the place at which he had fallen asleep the previous night.

Just then, G.R. ran his fingers though his thinning hair and he noticed that something was on his head. He ripped the object off his ears and instantly his hearing was back. He could hear birds chirping and water flowing in the nearby river.

He was now fully awake and his other senses were returning as well.

At that instant he held his nose.

Gingerbread, peppermint, cinnamon? What is going on? he thought. How could all these smells be coming from one place?

Right then, G.R. almost fainted as he saw the worst thing of all. He walked over to a 'for sale' sign that was all too familiar.

This was his sign. The sign that revealed his bar was coming. The sign that kept unwanted guests out. The sign that showed this foreign land was really not foreign at all.

But now his sign had a wreath around it.

How could this happen? When I went to sleep the ground was covered in filthy water and trash.

There wasn't a new tree in sight and the whole place smelled worse than a dirty diaper.

Could it have been that moose and the rest of those no-good kids? Impossible, they couldn't have done all this in just one night. This place must be haunted or something.

It was then that G.R. became aware of the worst thing of all. His face went as pale as the ghost of Christmas past and he had to lean against the 'for sale' sign so he didn't fall over.

"NOT NEW CAR SMELL!" he yelled.

Chapter 18

Cinnamon and new car smell
scare the bugs away...
Now Forest Noel can
come out and play.

Maury's Mickey Moose alarm sounded indicating that it was a new day.

Had last night been a dream? Maury thought as he rolled out of bed. It sure felt real.

Shutting off the alarm, Maury noticed the nutcracker on the night stand. A smile came across his face as he realized the nutcracker wasn't the only thing that was fixed last night. The smile remained on his face as he ate breakfast and walked to class.

"Quiet class," said Miss L. Toad. "Before we get to today's lesson, I have a very important announcement to make."

"A few days ago I regrettably informed you that the school Christmas party was cancelled. Well, it appears that things have changed, and Jingle Bell Block is now available for our party."

The class erupted with applause at the news. Page, Julia, Rob, Simon, Stock, Justine, Mikey and Maury looked at one another and smiled.

So that is our story about Forest Noel...
About an evil worm whose plan
to build a bar didn't end well.
Christmas was saved all thanks
to Maury and friends...
Who made sure that their
holiday tradition didn't come to an end.
There is a lesson to be learned
from this story we just told...
And it is something to be remembered
whether you are young, or you are old.
Next time you are in a bind,
think of Maury and his crew...
And know that when you put your mind to it,
there is nothing you can't do.

THE END

CPSIA information can be obtained
at www.ICGtesting.com
Printed in the USA
FSOW01n0732131115
13373FS